I0519668

WARNING

This book contains sexually explicit scenes and adult language. It may be considered offensive to some readers. This book is for sale to adults ONLY.

Please store your files wisely where they cannot be accessed by underage readers.

* * * * * * * * * * * * * * * * * * *

WANT FREE COPIES OF MY BOOKS?

Just visit my blog and download free copies of my books:

http://gideon-elliot.awesomeauthors.org/gideon-elliot/

Copyright © 2015 by Gideon Elliot

All Rights reserved under International and Pan-American Copyright Conventions. By payment of required fees you have been granted the non-exclusive, non-transferable right to access and read the text of this book. No part of this text may be reproduced, transmitted, downloaded, decompiled, reverse-engineered or stored in or introduced into any information storage and retrieval system, in any form or by any means, whether electronic or mechanical, now known, hereinafter invented, without express written permission of 4Fun Publishing. For more information contact 4Fun Publishing. The publisher does not have any control over and does not assume any responsibility for author or third-party websites or their content. This book is a work of fiction. The characters, incidents and dialogue are drawn from the author's imagination and are not to be construed as real. While reference might be made to actual historical events or existing locations, the names, characters, places and incidents are either products of the author's imagination or are used fictitiously, and any resemblance to actual persons living or dead, business establishments, events or locales is entirely coincidental.

About the Publisher

4Fun Publishing, a member of **BLVNP Incorporated**, 340 S. Lemon #6200, Walnut CA 91789, info@blvnp.com / legal@blvnp.com

NOTE: Due to the highly emotional reaction of some people to works of erotic fiction, any email sent to the above address that contains foul language or religious references is automatically deleted by our anti-spam software and will not be seen. All other communications are welcome.

DISCLAIMER

Please don't be stupid and kill yourself. This book is a work of FICTION. Do not try any new sexual practice that you find in this book. It is fiction and not to be confused with reality. Neither the author nor the publisher or its associates assume any responsibility for any loss, injury, death or legal consequences resulting from acting on the contents in this book. Every character in this book is over 18 years of age. The author's opinions are not to be construed as the opinions of the publisher. The material in this book is for entertainment purposes ONLY. Enjoy.

Gideon Elliot

Sweet Surrender

TABOO BUNDLE

Gay Bondage Erotica

Sweet Surrender

Taboo Bundle
Gay Bondage Erotica

By: Gideon Elliot

© **Gideon Elliot 2015**
ISBN: 978-1-62761-363-7

Sweet Surrender
Gay Bondage Erotica

GIDEON ELLIOT

STILL
LIFE

GAY ROMANCE

STILL LIFE

Mark took the cigarette away from his lips, slowly, with a gesture that had to indicate he was thinking hard about something. The room was in a half-light as the corners of night began to recede and the dust of dawn began to powder the sky. What was it he could not remember? That would be the key piece, the missing piece, he thought. The reason. What had he said? Everything was a blank.

It was nice anyway that whoever it was he had come home with had left him a pack of cigarettes and a box of matches -- and a slip of paper with a phone number on it and a name.

He had not had cigarettes by his bedside for over three years, and there he was, standing only in a pair of jeans by the window looking out at the falling snow smoking a cigarette. He rubbed his head and remembered the bar and the guy.

The guy from the bar left after Mark had passed out and he realized he'd been burned. That was not so long ago. But it was before Mark woke up and sat forlornly looking at daybreak.

Mark was gorgeous. That was the first thing Tayler had noticed when he saw him walk into a flood of rose light when he entered the bar. The exit sign was shining on the wall above the arch that framed him. He stood like a model on a runway.

Tayler let out a long sigh and wondered why a guy like that would get so fucked up. He shut the radio and blew out the candle by his bedside. Maybe it was from the beatings he'd told him about, the beatings he'd taken in the army from guys who couldn't overcome their need to ravish him. They wanted to possess his beauty, to be charged by his electricity. They were impelled by a force of desire they detested. Their desire turned to envy; envy turned to hatred; hatred gave way to disparagement, and disparagement became contempt. And so they beat him for his unworthiness.

"I understood that people were monsters who deserved only my sneers," Mark said to Tayler, enjoying his words and taking a long swallow of his vodka sour. He had just told him what happened to him in the army.

"Not always," Tayler said, not wanting Mark to be talking like that, wishing he were speaking of love not war, wishing to hear the tenderness he needed to hear in his voice.

"Not always," Tayler's words, hung between them.

"Always," Mark said, intransigent.

Tayler put his hand out and took hold of Mark's shoulder, stubbing out his cigarette in the thick glass ashtray on the bar with his other hand.

"You're really not so cynical are you?"

"I probably am," crossed Mark's mind, but the feeling of Tayler's hand on his shoulder had a content all its own that had nothing to do with what he was saying. Tayler felt the life pulsing inside Mark as he held Mark's shoulder. With his whole body, Mark said "welcome." Tayler felt it and drew near.

As if moved by the force only of desire, which had united their wills in one purpose, their lips met, their tongues touched, their breaths mingled. "I want to go home with you," Tayler said.

"Come," Mark said. "I want you inside of me." But it did not go that way.

Tayler would never take anybody in his sleep. He did not think of sex that way. Nor did he think of it as making love, a phrase that just about embarrassed him. Sex was simply being with someone, you and him, knowing the thrilling quietness of a mutual humanity.

He looked at Mark, sprawled over him in only a pair of black satiny mini-boxers. He extricated himself, kissed him lightly on the temple and covered him and quietly, lit a cigarette, scribbled his coordinates, forgot the pack on the side table, and let himself out. Mark found his note and melted when he read it. Tayler's sweetness filled his words. His words had the life of his body in them.

Now Mark remembered sitting with him in the rose light of the bar fascinated by the determination in his green eyes. His jaw was set, too. He was comfortable with himself, at home in his own skin. Mark wanted to claw at him. His body only became calm when Tayler touched him. He snuffed out the cigarette. And shook his head. No, there was no risk of that. That was that. He brushed his teeth and gargled.

He picked up the piece of paper on the night-table as he passed his bed, only a towel around him, went into the living-room, and unplugged his cell phone from the charger. He woke Tayler up.

"I'm sorry," he said.

"For what?" Tayler said.

"Falling asleep," Mark said sheepishly.

Oh," Tayler said. "I thought it might be for waking me up."

"I'm sorry for that, too," Mark said with a little dark purr in his voice. "I'll call back later. If that's ok."

"No, no, it's ok. I'm up now. Stay on. Why are you calling? Not just to apologize?"

"No," Mark said. "I want to see you again. I want to make it up to you."

"You want to make it up to me?"

"Yeah."

"Is that all?"

"I still want you inside me. Maybe I want to make it up to myself, too."

"Meet me at the waterfront this afternoon."

"Can't."

"You can't?"

"It's not that I don't want to. I teach. How about tonight? Is later tonight, around nine good? So I can get myself together. You can come over for dinner."

"I'd rather go out."

They met on St. Mark's Place outside The Taberna, a Greek place that Mark knew. It had begun to snow. They both arrived in front of the restaurant at the same time and embraced. No one had to wait outside in the cold for the other, stamping his feet.

"It's good to see you. I'm really sorry about last night," Mark said, a lovely smile gracing his face. But Tayler was not having it and told him he had nothing to apologize for although he might have a lot to think about.

"Like what?" Mark asked without rancor.

Tayler drew in his breath. "Like what you keep avoiding."

"What's that?"

"I don't know," Tayler said. "It just seems to me you are trying to blank something out."

You're so analytical," Mark said gently taking Tayler's cheeks in his palm and drawing his lips to him.

"Not here," Tayler said.

"And why not here?" Mark said.

"Look at your menu."

"Octopus."

"Octopus?"

"I like it," Mark said. "And vine leaves. They're good here."

So they both had a vinegar drenched grilled octopus and stuffed vine leaves and Tayler liked them. But he was easy to please, anyhow.

"Will you go with me next Friday night?" Mark said.

"You know what you're doing?"

"Yeah, being who I am. Openly, as they say."

Tayler shrugged. Outside, the snow had begun to fall again.

"Why else you want me to go?"

"Because I'm starting to feel like I need to be with you all the time. I'm complete only when I'm with you. Otherwise I'm missing something. Do you feel that way about me?"

"Do you think I'd surrender that kind of information to a sadist like you?"

"Torture will open your lips."

"So will kisses," Tayler said coming closer.

"In that case," Mark said, but the rest of his words were smothered in a kiss.

They were like two Greek warriors horsing around, wrestling with each other on the plains of Troy. Naked, their bodies glinted bronze in the evening light. They looked as if they were still clad in breastplates. As the blazing sun inched its orange-saturated ball downwards, it fell behind the distant jagged mountains. Then it became impossible to distinguish between rock and the ether.

They strained their muscles in the simultaneous effort to seize and to evade until the force of the power that strove through them brought their lips together and the kiss only intensified their struggle.

Tayler gave an open-throated yawn and squeezed Mark's hand as they walked through the chill air of Manhattan in December.

"I love you," Mark said.

"It's mutual," Tayler said. He meant it, but he was pessimistic. The surface often has a way of disappearing leaving you stuck somewhere that isn't anywhere. He looked at Mark.

"You don't believe me?" Mark said, stopping in his tracks and turning a full half circle so that he was facing him

"I don't know what to believe."

"Believe what I tell you."

"Yes, Sir," Tayler said with a grin, snapping to attention. Mark leaned over and the warm breath of his whisper taunted Tayler's neck. "I really mean it," he said.

"Time has a way of changing meaning," Tayler said with soft sadness in his voice. "And desire has a way of vanishing in time."

"Do you expect yours will?"

"I don't know."

They walked a little in silence until Tayler took Mark's hand. "Now it's my turn," he said, "to ask for forgiveness."

"For what?" Mark said, truly puzzled.

"For being a wet blanket."

"Wet as you are, I'd love to crawl under you. Come home with me. We can have some hot rum and you can fuck me. I'm starting to feel you inside me already." Tayler spotted a cab and hailed it. They sped through the city and got out in the urban pastoral of a snow-swept Washington Heights.

"I want it to be always like this," Mark said, his arm wrapped around Tayler's bare shoulder, looking into his eyes. Always."

Tayler nodded his head and smiled wistfully, fleetingly and then kissed Mark gently on the lips. He understood that he was committing himself to something that was sure to get out of his control.

End of the 1ˢᵗ book

GIDEON ELLIOT

THREE
TRANSFORMATIONS
GAY ROMANCE

THREE TRANSFORMATIONS

I was shy about my body. I was ashamed of the lust I felt for it, apparently so unjustified. I was ashamed of the image of myself I coveted, that I kept secret -- a well-toned, well-contoured, lean body, rippling with muscles, and graceful. Ease of body -- I wanted it, I envied it, I did not have it. And I couldn't help looking at guys who did. With infinite, inexpressible longing, a longing that broke my heart.

Sometimes I showed my obsession with my body by letting it go to pot, eating badly, not exercising, not paying too much attention to hygiene or how I dressed. This kind of neglect shows contempt for the body that is borne out of a sense of despair at one's own insufficiency. But moods change; cycles end; new ones begin. The moon fulfills and extinguishes itself.

I had fallen into a troth, a slough of despond, but I had pulled myself out, even while nothing around had changed -- I still lived alone, spent a lot of time inside my head trying to make myself feel that although imagination was not experience, perhaps experience might be conjured through its exercise.

I knew from the first moment I saw him that I could have him doing anything I told him to do in a matter of weeks. I liked the way he looked. I got off on the idea that I could make him look better. I could shape him, own him, become his god. The blasphemous thought made me shudder with a nervous excitement.

He looked at the locker like he'd never seen one, grasped the handle and slowly opened the door. He pulled his clothes off and stuffed them inside the locker. Instead of underwear, he was already wearing a bathing suit. He looked ok in it. A little black speedo. He walked out to the pool. I followed him.

"That's not all you come here for," I said. He was startled. Good.

"Not just to swim," I said. "But to work out. Seth," I said, introducing myself.

"Adam," he said. "You're right. I'd let myself go," he explained, "and I'm trying to get back in shape."

"You're doing ok," I said.

After a swim, we went into the work-out room, only the two of us. The hour had gotten late.

"Let me see you do some push-ups," Adam said. "At least fifty." I hesitated, but felt comfortable and then did not hesitate, and did ten.

"Not bad," he said, "not bad form, but ten. What's that? I said fifty." With formal perfection, grace and elegance, he easily did fifty. "Your turn now. Go ahead," he said coaxingly. I did.

Adam was working as hard as he could to please me, and he was doing a pretty good job of it, and whenever I let him know it, he just began to shine with happiness.

"I like to see you sweat," I said. "I like the way it makes your muscles glisten. You become so smooth." I slid my palms over his bare chest, "so...slippery."

He sighed and collapsed in gentle surrender, leaning his body into mine. Our chests stuck together and we radiated the energy we'd accumulated in our work-out. It had not taken great effort to take hold of him, and now, I possessed him completely. I could make him do whatever I wished. He pushed himself hard for me.

***

I WAS not going to let any of it get to me. That was what I told myself. That was my resolve. I was not going to let barriers be barriers or obstructions prevent me. I would master the circumstances and come out successful. Needless to say, there were numerous obstructions. But that firmed me in my resolve. I understood, if I let this go wrong, there would be nothing else after that. And I am not the sort who is good at dealing with nothing. I am not God, able to make something out of nothing.

Nearly every characteristic of every one of the young people was an obstruction. The boys showed an arrogant politeness; the girls, a brazen shyness. My colleagues, too, were an obstacle, my colleagues with their southern-fried iciness, the chilling warmth that had as its only real purpose the ability to freeze you to the bone until you learned to give it back. I lived in the blue heat of isolation. Every night, I sat late at my desk after preparing lessons, wondering how I had gotten myself into this. That was idle reverie, but in the cold hot climate I needed something to keep me warm. And that was it. And it was easier to think about that than to wonder how I was going to get out.

Even I understood, tremblingly, that my nebulous resolutions to succeed were very likely ill-founded. They were not becoming actual. So it was something like whistling in the dark to say I was not going to let barriers be barriers. I was daunted by obstructions, blocked by obstacles, stymied by forces that confined me, by currents I felt, but was unable to see. It was obvious, I was incompetent at my job. I was weak when it came to keeping order. Pandemonium was the rule in my classes. Nothing I did worked. Not scolding, lecturing, quietly waiting, cajoling, being a good fellow, being harsh. Nothing.

I knew everyone knew it, just from the looks everyone gave or did not bother to give. I knew I was of no account. It was only a matter of months before the year was over and I would be out, out. No chance of renewal. If there was anything that made the days tolerable, well, it would be better to say, if there was anyone who made the days tolerable, it was Farrell Whitney. He taught mathematics, Greek, and was the boys' swimming coach.

I felt, although we had hardly spoken and he was not in any way an outsider, as I was, I felt nevertheless, that there was a hidden bond between us, that he saw through me, understood me, appreciated me, could see that I was not the person I appeared to be, so singularly insignificant, but that there was something to be regarded, although it was not apparent to a common gaze.

I don't know why I should have this sense. Perhaps because of something in his gaze, something that invited confidence although I had never known how to begin a conversation. It took the day I was let go, something not altogether unexpected given the impossibility of my performance at the school, for the bond that I had sensed between Farrell and me to show itself as something more than a disturbance of my imagination.

I was walking back to the staff lodgings wondering where I would sleep that night. I had been given until week's end to clear out, but remaining on campus could only constitute deeper humiliation than going. So, I imagined I would put up at a cheap motel and figure it out, or at least try to, from there.

Farrell approached me, walking towards me across the campus green, a mottled sky behind him. "Graham," he said, using my name and addressing me for the first time in all our acquaintance or, really, our non-acquaintance. I knew he knew. I looked at him without speaking.

"It won't be the end of the world."

"No, I suppose not," I said.

"This isn't the time or place for it," he said. "Look, come to dinner tonight. My last class ends at four and I'll pick you up and any of your things. You can stay over the night at least." He had a house off-campus. I knew that.

"That's very kind of you, especially since you hardly know..."

He did not let me finish. "None of that," he said, blushing. "Be ready at four."

At four, I was standing at the school gate. "Get in," he said. "Stow your suitcase in the wayback."

It was all I had, that suitcase. I opened the hatch, slammed it down and got in the front beside him. He drove through the woods that lead away from the school, away from the gate towards the road and pulled at his tie with one hand and undid his shirt button.

"Any plans?" he said

"No," I answered.

"You probably don't have much money either."

"Enough to get by for a year if I'm careful."

"No place to stay."

"Right."

"Motels?"

"That's depressing."

"I'll put you up." I looked at him, but he kept his eye on the road. "It'll save you money."

"I can't do that."

"Why not?"

"It would be…," I began.

"...a relief not to worry about how you were going to get along," he said.

"I guess so," I said, "but, I can't do that. It's too..."

"You tend to argue a lot don't you?" he said. "That's why you're at this pass now." I said no more. He turned into a driveway and pulled up beside a two story Tudor style place.

"It's big enough," he said. "Come on in." I got out and followed him, but he turned back to me. "Don't forget your bag," he said. I went back to the car and took my suitcase out and wheeled it along the brick path. We went in by the side door. It was a big place with quite a bit of land around it.

"It was part of a larger plantation," Whitney said. "But they've all been divided up. Too much for anybody to keep up without slaves."

"You almost sound wistful," I said.

"No," he said. "I'm not." I looked at him. "You don't believe me," he said.

"No, I do," I said. "It just sounded..."

"I'm not wistful," he said. "I get what I want."

I did not know what that meant, and I did not know what to say. So I remained silent and followed him into the house, into a large kitchen. From there, we climbed an enclosed stairway up to the second floor. I followed him down a narrow corridor. He threw open a door and revealed a large room with a four poster bed, an oak dresser, a straight-backed chair, and an oak desk.

"Why are you doing this?" I asked.

"Call it Southern hospitality," he said and winked. "The bath tub's over there. Take off your clothes and follow me," he said walking away from me down the long, narrow hall. He turned into the bathroom and began to run the water into the tub.

This is strange, I thought, but I did not object. There was nothing menacing in his attitude, nothing at all. Still dressed, I followed him.

"What's...?"

He did not let me finish but put a finger gently to my lips. "Call it a purification ritual," he said, "ridding yourself of the past and inviting the future. Take off your clothes." I did, and laid them on a table in the bathroom. "Get in," he said, inviting me to step into the tub, when I stood before him naked. I obeyed without speaking. I stepped into the tub and lowered myself into the embrace of mildly hot water.

"Stand up," he said.

I stood. Slowly he began to lather me with soap in long soapy strokes from my heels to the fork of my body. Then with strength he did not withhold, he caressed my chest, and with soapy hands he took my scrotum in his palm and laved it. Then he brushed soap strokes on my cock, which had already risen and was standing hard and straight. He took it within his fist, looked at me with clear delighted eyes and said, "mine."

***

LOCKE PIERSON stood by the parapet of the penthouse terrace idly scanning the park with the telescope that was usually pointed at the heavens.

"Find anything?" Crane said, handing him a vodka and tonic.

Locke looked up, took the drink, smiled his entrancing smile, tipped his glass in jaunty greeting, and they both took long swallows of their drinks and felt the excitement of the alcohol rush through them. Their flesh magnetized and drew them together.

"I wasn't really looking," Locke said. "But I did find something," he said. "Look." A boy, in his late teens, it appeared, was sprawled on the steps at the Bethesda fountain.

"So?" Crane said, looking sideways at Locke.

"You are particularly adorable when you are obtuse," Locke said, putting his arm round Crane and pulling them nearer each other.

"Oh," said Crane. "I thought your days of picking up strays were over."

"Don't be bitchy," Locke said, his lips nearly brushing Crane's as he spoke. Their breaths touched first. Then their lips brushed and stuck. They dived into the ocean of a kiss but quickly broke water before the sea tide could take them out very far. "Sorry," Locke said.

"Don't mention it," Crane answered with the slightest show of petulance. "It still feels good."

"Don't go there," Locke said.

Locke took another swallow of his drink and finished it. He handed the empty glass to Crane. "One more for the road?" he said.

"I'm glad you stopped by," Crane said.

"And you're glad I'm going," Locke said.

"Buzz will be home soon," Crane said sheepishly.

"Right, Buzz. So no drink?" Locke said.

"Not this time. Next time?"

"Next time," Locke said. "When's that?"

"Surprise me," Crane said.

"Don't I always?" Locke said

"Are you going into the park?" Crane asked

"Might," Locke said.

"Take care, Locke. It really was good to see you."

"Sure. So long."

***

THE KID was still sprawled on the steps, a knapsack next to him, when Locke passed him apparently on his way down to the fountain. Although it had begun to drizzle, the boy looked like he was not moving from the spot.

"You're going to get wet," Locke said, stopping beside him.

"So will you," the kid said.

"But I intend to get out of the rain. It doesn't look like you do."

"It won't rain long."

"Don't you have any place to go?"

"What's it to you?"

"Nothing," Locke said. "Just concerned."

"About what?"

"Somebody down on his luck."

"What makes you think I'm down on my luck?"

"Because you're sprawled on the steps in the rain and it looks you got no place to go."

"Yeah," the kid said. "I guess you've got a point."

"You want to go for a coffee?"

"You trying to pick me up?"

"You could say that."

"You don't have somebody regular."

"Nope."

"Ok."

"Fuck the coffee, man. If you want take me home with you, as you yourself just said, I got no place to go."

"Pick up your junk," Locke said. "But as far as I'm concerned you can leave it."

He gathered his stuff together and bunched it tight in the blanket he'd been sitting on. "We gotta find some place where I can ditch this shit."

"Put it down in that corner."

"Now where are you gonna take me?" the young man asked, hooking his palm over Locke's arm.

"Home."

"Where's that?"

By now they were by the curb and Locke's arm was out and a cab stopped for them.

"First Street off Second Avenue."

The apartment was made of two interconnecting floors in an old tenement that had been redone. They were painted white and sparsely furnished.

"Get into the bath tub, you little beggar," Locke cried roughly, tossing him a fluffy white towel, which he caught.

"Get out of those filthy clothes and get into the tub."

"What are you going to do?" Stuart said as he pulled his t-shirt over his head after Locke snapped his fingers because he had not immediately heeded him.

He was a very sweet. Locke soaped him very gently and made him shine in his smiling, naked beauty. Locke touched his lips with his fingers and without even thinking about it, Stuart kissed the fingers his lips touched. They gazed into each other's eyes. Both understood what had happened. Locke had taken him and he had surrendered.

Stuart lay naked on the bed in the glow of half a dozen wax candles, drifting high and deep, awake and sweetly stoned. Locke in slow motion dragged his tongue over his nipples, making them tumescent as he blew cool breath on them and stroked his abs and then went lower and took him from under the scrotum and caressed him with the undulating pressure of his palm. He rubbed the crown of his cock the tender glans and made him crazy with desire. He raised himself up and kissed him on the mouth and knew he owned him by the way he surrendered to the kiss.

End of the 2nd book

GIDEON ELLIOT

THREADS

GAY ROMANCE

THREADS

Terry passed by the loungers along Central Park West. Young men and men hoping to look young leaned against a waist-high stone wall, behind them the park and its abundant foliage, its stately and many-branching trees, its darkness.

They looked with disdainful stares at most of the passersby. They waited for a perfection they would never know or achieve despite their peacocking. Terry yearned, unable to focus on what it was he was thinking. Nor could he feel the desire that he knew was his.

"Can't catch the threads of my thoughts. Don't know where they're going. When I try to follow them, they are gone, slithered away before I get hold of them. Clouds in the sky, drift out of shape and disappear, are less elusive than my thoughts."

The anxiety of excitement determined his pace. He walked too fast, as if he were trying to desert the place he longed to inhabit. He could not look into the eyes of the men he longed to gaze upon. The night was hot. He was uncomfortable wearing the tight sleeveless t shirt and cut away jeans he had put on for this walk when he imagined it. He longed for it, and dreaded that someone might approach him. He had wanted to make himself seen and desired and now he felt alien and wished he were invisible. His feet were perspiring and clammy in his sandals. He had wanted so badly earlier, and now he was fleeing from his want.

"You waste your time like that?" she said discharging smoke after a big draw on her extra-long cigarette. "Night after night. What kind of life is that? Where is it…where are you…going? You're taking a walk, out to lunch, waiting for someone to feed you."

"This is fruitless," he answered.

"You will be fruitless, achieve nothing, if you don't start being serious about what you are going to do. Remember the story of the grasshopper and the ant."

He laughed.

"It's not funny."

"Well, it is," he said, still laughing.

"You are impossible," she said, "you worry me, and if you were not so charming, and my son...give me a kiss." He complied. "There's more duty in that than genuine affection," she said. "Try again." He kissed her again. "That's better," she said.

It really was not, but she pretended that it was, as she always did.

***

IT WAS around eight in the morning, Terry got home from doing the night shift at the bakery where he worked at the same time that Jason would bound down the stairs of the brownstone where they split an apartment. He was on his way to his office, impeccably groomed, as usual, almost unrecognizable if you had only seen him in his leather-drag.

"Good morning," Terry, he said, as they passed each other at what they came to call the changing of the guard.

"Larry stayed over last night, so don't be surprised if he's padding around in the kitchen and uses the shower," Jason said. "He has an audition at ten."

In fact, Larry was already up and sitting at the kitchen counter, gingerly sipping a burning cup of coffee, unsweetened, strong, black.

"None for me thanks. I'm hopped up enough and ought to get some sleep," Terry said as Larry looked up and undifferentiating it from his greeting extended a cup to him. "I have an audition this morning."

"Jason told me. I passed him in the hall," Terry said.

"West Side Story. Patrick," Larry said mock preening.

"No kidding!"

"I'm ready."

"I bet."

"Wanna come along?"

"What about my sleep?"

"Later. There's always time for that, but you are young only once."

Instead of bed, consequently, Terry took a power shower: hot water, soap, hard scrub, shave, shampoo, hot rinse, cold rinse. Tingling he stepped into his bedroom and got into an old, soft, faded pair of jeans and a loose button-down-the-front, white shirt, ivory, actually, its short sleeves rolled up several times, old ivory buttons mostly unbuttoned over a chest he had been working on.

"Don't ask me if I feel self-conscious. I am determined to get over that. I'm through with trying to disappear and not to be seen, when all I really want is to be looked at," he said when Larry opened his eyes big and raised eyebrows at the sight of him. But all he said when he saw him was, "Sleek."

"Nothing compared to you," Terry said. They were not dressed very differently. Larry wore a skin-tight orange t shirt that showed his torso off to perfection. It was obvious which one of them had the charisma.

"I was not mistaken," Terry said later that evening, "watching Larry on stage. I was in the back of the theater. I could see the producers thought as highly of him as I did. And they had good seats."

When he was offered the part two mornings later, he took it.

"You are on your way," Jason said when Larry told him.

Over the following weeks, Larry became so immersed and involved in his new role that the rest of the world shrunk considerably. He withdrew from it. He disappeared, Jason said.

"He's working," Terry said.

"Well, of, but what will become of me?" Jason said. The charm of his pout and of the whimper inside which he wrapped the word "me" was exponentially amplified by the fact that he was wearing a pair of tight leather jeans, boots, and was bare-chested. He was chiseled. Terry had never seen him without a top on, and he did not know until he saw the silver rings that threaded through them that Jason's nipples were pierced. "Play with your nipples," Terry said.

"I'm serious," Jason said.

"So am I," Terry said. "What else can you do?"

"Play with yours," he said, taking hold of Terry and drawing him to him, by his nipples.

"You are kinky," Terry said.

"Shut up," Jason said, slapped him, and then took him in a kiss. When he let go Terry moaned and sighed and his mouth grabbed up at Jason's and brought him back into him.

"You're still not him," Jason said as they came down.

"No," Terry said. "I can't be."

"So what good is it?"

"Thanks," Terry said, patting his cheek.

"I don't mean that," Jason said, pressing himself harder into him, softer but hardly soft.

"I actually do understand," Terry said, "and I respect it. We are such stuff as moments are made on."

Jason slowly began to withdraw. Terry sighed. Afterwards they went down into the street together. The city was crowded the way it is when everyone pours back into it after escaping for the summer. New York was having a warm September.

"Let's go in there," Jason said pointing to the newly opened Black Slumber. Unlike the majority of gay bars, it did not have pounding techno music. When they entered the darkened environments, there was a cd of the Bach unaccompanied cello suites playing. Despite this cultural anomaly, the place was full. Tables were all taken and there was no room at the bar. Jason managed, nevertheless, to secure them two vodka martinis. They stood in a throng near a closed-off, no longer used doorway.

"If you are smart," Terry said, "you will push yourself out of the picture and concentrate on being available for Larry, even if he does not avail himself much of your availability. That is if you want to keep him. This is just the point at which your whole thing could break up and it's up to you." He paused and then added, "If you want him."

"I do," Jason sighed. "I want him."

"You are going to have to share him with a lot of people when he makes it big, which he will."

Terry was not wrong. The revival was a smash. Larry was a star.

"I guess that's it," Jason said, on a Sunday morning three months after the show opened.

"What's what?" Larry responded, puzzled and wary.

"Us."

"What about us?"

"Is there still an us?"

"What are you talking about?"

Jason had not heeded Terry's advice. It was a problem of boundaries. "Be one with me," Jason had had inscribed on the inside of a silver bracelet he had given Larry.

"In my love, I am," Larry said, "but we are separate, too." Jason did not like that.

"It is not love. It's ownership and control. That is not in my plan," Larry explained. "I am ambitious. I don't intend to sacrifice my ambition, which is paying off. This is the kind of thing that happens once in a life time and not to very many."

"You'd make a great submissive," Jason said.

"Don't count on it," Larry said.

"I did not expect this," Larry said, sipping his coffee. "And I don't need it now."

"I understand," Terry said.

"What do you understand?" Larry said. "Say what you think."

"I think I understand you. It's an amazing time for you. You are the star of a great Broadway musical."

"I'm the same person I've always been," Larry protested.

"I did not say you were not."

"But I'm very busy, and I have to be rested and fit every night."

"You don't have to tell me this."

"What don't you understand?"

"I did not say I didn't understand anything. I said I did, both you and Jason."

"What about Jason?"

"He's jealous."

"For Chrissake."

"He is."

"Or does he just want to sabotage everything just when I make it? Jealous my ass. He's jealous of losing control. He's not kidding when he talks about wanting me to become a submissive. But no thanks. If he can't love my success, I'm sorry. I love him, but I'm not going to give up on what I want."

"Despite everything you love him?"

"Yes."

"I have an idea."

Then, in the midst of so much inevitable, ubiquitous, unnecessary drama, there was a week-long strike by the stagehand's union and Broadway went dark. Larry was terribly conflicted. He supported the stagehands, but he was itching to perform. In addition, no one knew, as it was in process, how long the strike would take. The strike might end at any moment or go on past all endurance.

Larry was on edge with eagerness, anticipation, boredom, and frustration. He could not relax and go about each day as if it were a designated piece of a defined vacation, for example. He was irritable and cranky. He snapped at Jason and Terry or ignored them when he was at the apartment until Jason lost it.

"What are you doing here?" he shouted at Larry who had just complained that everything he touched was dirty. They were around the table. Terry had made dinner, a fish soup, a roast chicken, mashed sweet potatoes, and sautéed green beans and tomatoes.

Larry had chided him for serving fish soup and chicken as parts of the same meal since they were so uncomplementary.

Terry did not agree with him, but he did not rebut him. Terry did not care and he knew that Larry did not, really, either: Larry was all tense inside with nerves; he was always ready and waiting to get back onstage.

"Would you rather I not be here?" Larry turned angrily to Jason, showing his teeth, which, although they really were beautiful, were disturbing to look at now for the fierceness they conveyed. "If you are going to hover like a black cloud, maybe," Jason answered.

"I can hardly believe you," Larry said, thinking of his need for people to keep him together, even to pamper him at a time like this, "considering…." He was at a loss for words, astonished, and taken up short.

"We all have situations," Jason said, "and that does not mean we can go around dumping our shit on everybody else."

Terry could see Larry holding himself back. He was in superb shape, a singing actor who danced modern ballet. He stood to go. Jason sat frozen, suddenly unable to comprehend how it had come to this. It was not where he would have taken it. Yet, it was he, precisely, who did take it there.

Terry stood up, too, and walked out of the dining room with Larry, as if he were seeing him to the door and mollifying animosity. "Remember what I suggested a few weeks ago?" he said, sotto voce before he opened the door. "Now's the time. It's not fair, but he's in worse shape than you."

"You did not leave," Jason said, looking at Larry as they reentered the dining room and took seats again.

"You are more on edge than I am," Larry said.

"I can't live without you. I'm going to pieces."

"You are not living without me."

"You are never here for me anymore, since the show began, and now that there's a strike, you are like someone nervously occupying a waiting room."

"Can you care for me when I'm like that? Even when I rebuff you? This is important to me."

"I can only promise to try," Jason said.

"That's a toast," Terry said, took three glasses out of the closet and poured three shots of cold vodka, but into Jason's he poured a harmless soporific as well, and Jason fell asleep sprawled out, as he was, on the couch.

When Jason awoke, he was tied, naked, chained spread-eagle to the four posts of his bed.

"You spiked my vodka," he said looking at Terry.

"Yes, I did," Terry said.

"Where's Larry?" Jason asked. "Why can't I move?" Just then, Larry emerged from the bathroom dressed as he would be were he onstage as Patrick. "You have been a real ass-hole," he said, "a selfish ass-hole." He stood over Jason immobilized, and just as he finished his last reprimand, he slapped Jason.

"What are you doing?" Jason said condescendingly.

"Teaching you a lesson in humility and regard for others, especially when they are others who you claim to love and adore and cherish."

"What have I done?" Jason said as if he were trying to demonstrate to Larry that he ought to be reasonable.

"Open your mouth," Larry ordered.

Without a thought, before he could think, Jason did, and Larry immediately pushed a leather ball gag into his mouth and fastened the straps attached to it in order to keep it in place behind Jason's head. When Jason tried to speak, the way the gag pressed on the back of his throat elicited the gag reflex. Jason realized he was more comfortable the less he exercised his throat.

"Good," Larry said. "You know how to follow orders. Automatically."

He pressed the point of a pin against Jason's nipple. Jason flailed. His cock was hard. Terry thumbed the base of his perineum right below where the titanium ring circled the base of his cock and the underside of his balls. Jason writhed. He bucked within himself when Larry inserted a dildo with a prostate stimulator at its end into him, fastened his cock in a leather pouch snapped on to a leather belt around his waist, and clipped his nipples with tiny clips that caused a sensation that teasingly mingled pleasure and pain.

They left him there alone. He feared it would be all night. At three, however, they came back carrying candelabras. They put their candelabras down. Jason saw them gaze at each other. He saw them kiss. They rubbed their naked bodies against each other. The softness of their lips was the entrance to bliss. They worshipped each other unto the crystallization of joy. Jason in the candle light watched as they became each other's shadow.

It bothered him that Larry was unavailable. He was jealous. He had raged within; he regretted it; he repented it. He had thought only of himself without regard for Larry. It had tormented him to see that Larry enjoyed the ever-flowing mass-gaze centered on him; that theaters full of people gazed on him, cared for him, desired him, were aroused when he walked onto the stage.

But fame was not what moved Larry. He had to do what was the source of his profoundest pleasure, the pleasure of being to the fullest by becoming a role he was playing. That excluded Jason and in it he loomed larger than he was in private with Jason. It was pure self-reliance. It was independence. Jason hated it. He wanted Larry to need him.

Night was thinning; particles of the shining gray were becoming blue. Jason had lain in darkness and was glad to see the morning's blue. The discord between what he had been and what he was now did not dissolve. He was trapped by torment and resignation. He had been humbled without being cleansed.

When they released him and removed the ball gag, he did not move or speak. He lay spent and drained, lost, unhappy, abandoned, wishing that he had not been freed. The torment of desire that had preceded his punishment had been slight compared to what was churning within him now.

If only now his torment were the work of someone else and not himself, he might find some relief.

End of the 3rd book

GIDEON ELLIOT

BROKEN HEARTS

GAY ROMANCE

BROKEN HEARTS

There was a banging on the door that threatened to interrupt the strange ceremony that was taking place. Michael was unfazed. He signaled to David to get the door, and keep whoever it was waiting in the entrance.

"He can't hear you," he said, coming back to me, smiling at my efforts.

It was true. I was begging him but Evan stood in front of me entirely inattentive, as if he were absorbed by something else far away going on deep inside himself. I could not tell. All I could tell was that physically present as he was, he was not there. He could not hear me. He could not see me either even though he was looking straight at me.

"Don't let him do that to you," I said, but to no avail. I wanted to shake him, but I was unable to reach over and touch him when I tried.

"There really is no point. You'll only wear yourself out. I suggest you resign yourself to the facts of life. He is not suffering. Look at him. You're feeling much more pain right now than he is," Michael said.

Something was truly diabolical about this man, this Michael (the militant archangel, become malignant, fallen, inhabiting the burning lake). He had come to have so much, too much, influence over my friend. The diabolical was not just an aspect of his spirit.

Physically, he resembled the iconographic cliché that has become the standard caricature of the devil. He was wearing a red smoking jacket over a black turtle neck, black leather jeans and boots. His spiked hair had more red in it than brown. His face was long. His chin was shaped by a pointy goatee. His eyes were green and flashing. His wrists were long and thin; his hands, graceful; his fingers, long and tapered. He could have been a pianist or a violinist. His voice was mellifluous. He varied his speech with the intonations of somebody who has perfect pitch. He blew the thick smoke from his Turkish cigarette out through his nose.

It was best not to argue, I thought. My task now was to get myself out of there safely and mentally intact.

"I don't want to wait." The shouting came from the entrance way and it was followed by a young man in a wool cap, a lumber jacket, a pair of dirty jeans and motorcycle boots barging into our room.

"Would you like to make love to him once more," Michael taunted me as this fierce visitor plunged into the room, "for old time's sake?"

"The way he is now?"

"He looks pretty good to me."

"But he's not here."

"No?"

"How long you gonna keep me waiting. I come. I pick up the package. I go. I don't wait," the intruder thundered.

"You will now," Michael said. The stranger, in fact, became silent and still.

"Not himself, no; he is not here, not his whole being," I said, defiantly, seething at something, at his arrogant assertion of power. It was all the more hateful because it was successful.

"Whoever is?" he answered as if he were parodying Oscar Wilde. "Furthermore," he added, "who knows really what that is, the whole being?"

"Speciousness and sophistry," I sneered.

"My, my," he mocked. "Don't be a prude. I'm offering you something you know you want."

He was right about that. "But not under these circumstances," I said.

"What other circumstances are there?" he challenged, trumping my objection. "But, suit yourself," he said amiably and turned to the young man in the lumber jacket who was quietly waiting.

"I was not sure what suited me anymore."

"Now if you wait here a moment," Michael said to him, "I will bring you the package and you can be on your way."

"Yes, sir. Thank you, sir," the motorcycle messenger said.

Meanwhile, I was mesmerized watching Evan who just stood there like a statue in stone, buried in some character-transforming trance. He did not, actually, look like he was standing there but as if he had been stood there. It looked like there was nothing he could do on his own. He had become the essence of an object.

***

I WOKE up Saturday morning and my heart felt like there was a cold chain wrapped around it, locked tight. The morning was gray against the windowpane and the air was full of incipient sorrow which would fall from everything in the form of snow. I had lived with Evan for three years and I was shocked when he came in one evening not long ago grinning all over and blistering with happiness.

"I'm going to be a monk," he said.

"What?" I said, continuing to stir the pot of soup I was making.

"A monk."

"A monk?"

"Oh not like in a church -- a sex monk. I'm going to become a sex monk."

"What's a sex monk?" I screamed.

"I am going to devote my life to the service of sex."

"I thought you had done that already years ago," I said, teasing him, still not knowing what he was talking about and what the joke was, if it was a joke -- and if he was serious, well, then what?

"I'm serious," he said, not defiantly but with great calm.

"I'm not sure I know what you are talking about," I said slowly, suddenly feeling both numb and scared.

***

"YOU WERE unreachable," I said when he got back Sunday evening as we lay in each other's arms, our naked bodies pressed against each other, our eyes dancing with each other to the invisible sounds made by the wave lengths of our minds. "I wanted to touch you but I couldn't. Where were you?" I said.

His eyes took on a dreamy wistful glimmer. They had the sparkle of somebody who knows he is exactly where he should be. "I was nowhere. It was wonderful." His smile was its own presence and it lighted him up with its electricity. It sent tremors of energy jolting through me like a current, when it suddenly trembles along the tracks of the nerves after you've accidentally touched something charged.

"Am I going to lose you?" I said.

"That depends on you," he said, taking hold of my scrotum in the cup of his hand and bringing his mouth to mine and kissing me with a gentle intensity that put his soul in his lips and in mine. I stopped thinking and felt myself expand. I needed him inside me and stretched to him, and he moved his fingers inside me. I began to kiss him actively bringing my throat from the back of my mouth up to the front so that every kiss could voice my devotion. And he hardened and so did I.

As our passions wrestled with each other, he took the liquid from our kisses and slicked himself and faced me with his eyes and put himself all the way inside me and then teasing me went in and out of me, and as he did, with the fingers of the hand that was not caressing my neck, he played my cock as if it were a flute. Afterwards, we lay still in each other's arms gazing into one another's eyes. Until the phone interrupted us. It was Evan's cell on the side table.

"Yes sir," he said smiling.

"Yes, sir?"

"Yes, sir. I will sir." And then he hung up. My heart had begun to sink even before he said, "I'm not going to sleep here tonight."

I looked at him with incipient despair in my eyes.

"That. Is. Not. Going. To. De-phase. You." he said, tapping my chest with the point of his right index finger in emphasis.

***

MONTHS WENT by. Evan moved out. I saw much less of him than I ever had, but he still visited me. Those times, it was like he was on loan. But that did not matter. When I was with him, all the agony of not being with him disappeared.

His hair had been cropped short and covered his scalp like a cap of black feathers. He shaved only every fourth or fifth day. He wore tight-fitting sleeveless undershirts and smoked cigarettes. He was leaner than he had ever been. Carelessly, he blew the smoke at me. He knows I loathe tobacco smoke and smoking in general.

It did not faze me. I kissed him when his mouth was full of tobacco smoke, and I lit his cigarettes for him, getting the sting of tobacco on my lips and the dull smoke on my tongue, and then gave him the lighted cigarette.

***

I STAGGERED from the blow that Evan delivered, straight to my solar plexus.

"What did you do that for?" I said when I got my breath back.

"Do what?" he said grinning.

"Do what?" I cried in imitation. "Punch me in the gut."

"I didn't like the way you lit my cigarette."

"You didn't like the way I lit your cigarette and you punched me in the gut?"

"I want to toughen you up, fruit cake," he said stroking my cheek and looking at me with what seemed like true affection.

"What's got into you?"

"Not what. Remember? Who is the question."

I tried another tack. "Toughen me up!"

"You're too soft. I want you harder, tougher." He took hold of me by the jaw and fastened his eyes on mine as he spoke.

"What for?"

"I want to see you increase your tolerance for pain."

"Pain?" I said.

"Pain," he repeated.

"Why do you want to do that?"

"I think there's something incredibly sexy about a guy who can bear pain. It gives him a strength that is just very hot. It is even sexier when he can no longer bear it and begins to beg to be released and will bargain away anything, even himself."

"You don't sound like yourself anymore, Evan. This is Michael, not you."

"It's me, alright. You just don't know who I am anymore. Maybe you never did. And for sure you don't know who you are either." Before I knew it my face stung from his slap and I doubled over from another body blow to my middle. "But I'm going to help you find out," he said, smiling.

"How?" I said, as if we were in the middle of a conversation.

"Like this," he said, repeating the blow just as I was beginning to stand straight.

"Stop it, Evan," I cried when my breath came back.

"Say please," he said.

"Please."

"Say it louder." His words were accompanied by a blow. I was staggered.

"Please," I said.

In response he punched and punched again, once with each fist against my hard gut and chest. Whatever he'd said about my being soft was not true. I have a hard body. That's what I was thinking, I have a hard body, as he was hitting me.

"Evan, stop it. You loved me once."

He spat. "Maybe if you beg," he said, followed by more blows.

"Please, Evan, stop. I'm begging."

"Not good enough."

"What do you want?

"What good is it if I tell you and if you don't give it to me?"

"I will. I will, Evan, whatever you want. Only stop hitting me. Please."

***

ONCE I went back to the loft with Evan, Michael greeted me with a menacing smile but offered us herb tea. "It is so nice that the two of you could remain friends," he said. Evan smiled and took hold of my hand and squeezed it. "Not everyone would be capable of making such a transition so smoothly. I must congratulate you," Michael said. He kissed me on both cheeks and pressed me to him with a force that made me weak and dizzy. I wanted his arms around me desperately, even though I didn't.

When I woke up, there were candles burning all around me. I was in a chair looking at the bed Evan was lying in his full strong length. The ceiling was painted a midnight blue. It was punctuated by white points of paint signifying stars. I knew Evan was in a trance, but I was not sure what that meant. I was naked. I felt as if I were a spirit in his body. Helium had become his element. He hovered weightlessly, a consciousness without an identity, unformed, yielding, and receptive. His mind was clay to be shaped and reshaped, an infinitely malleable thing. The thought of it made me swoon. The pain of my loss covered my heart with grief.

When his nipples were pierced I felt him become like the coldness and elegance of marble. When the lash was made to caress his flesh, I felt his flesh become strong like smooth iron. When the barbed wire circlet was tattooed around the biceps of his left arm I felt the hot blood of his muscles pump through him and make his entire body stiffen. He was a void, his mind dispersed like the elongating forms of a cloud on their way to disappearance. He was bent on his knees – my knees? -- adoring the feet of the man who had transformed his life. I wanted to run from what I saw. It was like vinegar in my heart. But I watched drinking it in until it squeezed me with grief.

Michael snapped his fingers and I saw Evan look up and stand up. He was immobile, silent, staring, lost in waiting.

***

EVEN IN a crowded subway train, I can always make private contact with a guy. I had not done it for a while, since I had lived with Evan, but now that he was out of my life for the most part, I started again. I was successful my first time out. Sam was an architect. He had a place in Brooklyn Heights. He was standing by the window, looking out over the East River at Manhattan. He was quiet but determined, and he did not brook contradiction.

"You're a funny combination," he said.

"What do you mean?" I asked. I sat across from him in a deco leather chair holding a champagne glass in one hand and a joint in the other.

"I mean you aren't withdrawn. You're quite forward, actually. But unless I miss my guess, you're also very passive, even masochistic."

"I wouldn't go that far," I said.

"Nevertheless, you cannot resist the wish to be obedient."

I said nothing.

"It's ok," he said, motioning to me with a flutter of his index finger to join him at the window. I stood up and took a few steps towards him and handed him the joint. He put his arm round my shoulder and drew me to him. He inhaled and said through his teeth as he held the breath, "I'll take good care of you."

I still said nothing but I looked puzzled.

"You need to belong to a man. Can't you see that? I want to have complete control over someone, complete power over him. I know you know what I mean. I am offering to take complete control of you and complete responsibility for you. You must agree to it, desire it, and surrender yourself to me entirely."

I had to admit that what he said excited me. "But it scares me," I said.

"I like that it does. I want it to be that way. I want you to be frightened of me. I want you to fear me and to fear that you have not pleased me. I will be slow and gentle with you and teach you how to serve me and help you grow to love that fear and your slavery, and to love me as well as to fear and desire me. You will belong to me and you will trust me entirely."

"How can I know if you will not betray my trust or hurt me beyond measure?"

"You can't. Your trust can only be a matter of faith."

"A matter of faith."

"Of faith."

"In?"

"In me."

Evan, believe it or not, was jealous when I told him I was giving up my apartment to be Sam's full-time, total slave. "Michael's not going to like that," he said.

"Why should he care one way or the other?" I said, puzzled. "Besides," I said, "there's nothing he can do about it. You're under his spell, not me."

End of the 4th book

GIDEON ELLIOT

Anthony and Patrick

GAY ROMANCE

ANTHONY AND PATRICK

After a long flight from Paris, Anthony checked into a hotel room in San Francisco. It was a foggy Friday morning. Once in his room, he did not take off his clothes or pull down the covers. He dropped face down onto the bed and immediately fell into a heavy sleep. Much later, that night, he would meet Patrick for a drink at The Sun and Moon. Afterwards, well, he thought the chances were good. They had been corresponding by e-mail for nearly a year since the break-up, sharing both serious problems and erotic remembrances.

Patrick was getting back from Seattle. He taped a weekly news commentary there for the BBC. Since Alistair Cooke's death he had been assigned to do a version of the Letter from America. Anthony was in San Francisco ostensibly to give a lecture at Berkeley on Tolstoy. The reason he'd accepted the invitation was to have an excuse to visit Patrick. Things had been rocky during their last year together, but once Patrick had made good on his threat to leave if Anthony did not curtail his promiscuous excursions, things changed.

Anthony was by himself. The anguish he felt at the loss would not go away. Pick-up sex did not help. Anthony realized he wanted nothing more. Only Patrick. It was a shock. He absorbed it. The bottomless misery helped him to. He wrote to Patrick and was surprised and encouraged when his letter was answered. After a few weeks their correspondence became intimate. Their letters were intimate the way they had been intimate when they first felt the thrill of being with each other and became focused only on each other. The affinity was still there.

"I remember," Anthony wrote, "how you could make me get hard just by looking into my eyes." Patrick wrote back the famous five words Bogart said to Bergman in *Casablanca*. And they worked.

Anthony lifted himself off the bed. He had to rub his neck to get the stiffness out of it. The day was turning dusky. His head was muzzy. He pulled his shirt out of his pants and up over his head. He was pleased how he looked in the mirror when he saw himself after his head was free of his shirt.

"Good body for an old man," he kidded himself, running his palms down along his torso and hips.

He did not really consider forty-one old. Still, it sounded different from even thirty-eight, more ominous. But, surveying himself, Anthony thought, "I'd still go home with me if I saw me on the street." That excited him. He became hard. He began fingering himself with the sensitive tips of his fingers as if he were touching a recorder. He resisted. Save it for Patrick.

Stripped, he went into the bathroom and ran the shower as hot as he could take it. Standing under it, he let the heavy points of water beat on him. He stretched every kink out of his body. He soaped himself and rinsed himself. Then he stood in water as cold as he could stand—even a little colder than that. He was tight. He shaved. He did his toilet. He ordered vodka and fresh orange juice be brought up to him.

He opened the door. There was only a white towel tied around his waist. The look in the eyes of the young man at the door pleased him. He could not take his gaze off Anthony's smooth, well-wrought chest. Anthony smiled at him such a smile that he could have had the boy had he wanted, for the boy was ready to melt in his arms.

"Will there be anything else, sir?"

Anthony did not invite the boy to stay, as once he might have. He was waiting for Patrick. He gave the kid twenty dollars and a wink.

"Thank you, sir."

"Be good," Anthony said, gently closing the door.

He took his time getting dressed. He knew what Patrick liked, and Patrick knew what he liked. Patrick liked men in expensive, well-tailored suits with very sexy underwear when they finally got stripped down. Patrick himself was a leather slut. Those were his words. He used them ironically, but he also really meant them.

"I like to be rewarded," Anthony had written once, "and sometimes the only reward I am worthy of is punishment." Patrick knew that and he knew how to use it.

Anthony slapped his cheeks with some *Eau Sauvage*, readjusted his tie in the mirror by the door, stepped into the corridor, took the elevator down to the great marble lobby and turned onto the street through the grand revolving doors. The night was cool and strong. It had a latent energy that penetrated to the heart.

His cell rang. "Patrick!" he said with delight. "Where are you?"

"Anthony. I got stuck at a meeting. Now I'm going out for a few drinks with some of the guys."

"What meeting?" Anthony said, although he wanted to say, "Guys?"

"We stopped at the BBC to discuss where the Letter was going."

"But it's quarter to nine and I'm in the street on the way over to The Sun and Moon. We have a date."

"Sorry, kid. Business comes first. How 'bout midnight we meet there for a drink."

"But then, what about?" Anthony began to object.

"We don't have to do it at all, Anthony," Patrick said, "if it's gonna bend you out o' shape to accommodate me."

"No, no," Anthony said, "I want to see you."

"So, you can see me at midnight."

"Ok."

"Great. I got to go now. They're waiting for me. See you later."

"Later," Anthony echoed, his spirit slumping. He snapped the phone shut. When Patrick finally did show up, it was quarter after one. Anthony was in a bitter mood.

"I was just about to leave," he said.

"I'm not stopping you," Patrick said, kissing him on the cheek.

"I've been waiting an hour and a quarter."

"I'm here now. Do you want to go into a sulk and I'll leave, or can we enjoy ourselves?"

Anthony pursed his lips, furrowed his brow, and made a contrite face.

"It's been a while since we've seen each other," Patrick said, offering Anthony a warm smile as a reward for his success at overcoming himself.

"A little over a year," Anthony said.

"You're looking good," Patrick said.

"Thanks," Anthony said. "You look…it's beyond words…better than ever."

Patrick was as lean as ever, but with greater muscular definition and contour. His black leather pants seemed like a second skin, showing his long muscular thighs to advantage. His chest was perfect. His taut nipples pressed against the thin, skin-tight, snow-white fabric of his sleeveless tank top. He held his head high and his hair was luxurious and abundant. "My new life agrees with me," Patrick said light-heartedly and Anthony cringed at the implication.

"Was it really that bad?"

"Hiding what needs to be out in the open is never good."

"I did not know."

"It would not have mattered if you had."

"Why not?"

"You wouldn't have been able to accept it."

Anthony was silent.

"Are you getting laid?" Patrick asked.

"Not the way I like."

"How come?"

"I need you for that."

The night was cool and the air was moist as they drove through the dirt roads in the woods of Marin County. There was a rich moist smell of earth and trees, of brown and green in the air.

"I need you for a lot more than that," Anthony said, watching Patrick drive and gazing upon his silhouetted profile framed by the side window. Patrick remained silent as he drove. He turned on the radio just as a performance of the St. Matthew Passion was beginning.

"I loved you once," he said breaking the silence that resonated with Bach.

"How I have wanted to hear that. What about now?" Anthony hesitated to ask. When he overcame his fear, his voice was self-consciously shy.

"Now, that's a failed love."

"Can it be saved?"

"No. It's blessed and buried, the adumbration of another time. It's as inaccessible as one of last month's rainstorms. I have changed. I'm stronger and more definite. I'm not afraid to say it."

"Does that mean," Anthony asked, "that we cannot—I don't know how to say it."

"Be lovers, be partners? Not the way we were."

"It was my grandfather's," Patrick said of the house near the top of the steep hill they drove up. "It was strange. I came out here and a week after I visited he died. He was ninety-seven, but very much alive."

It was not a large house, but it was not small either. It was definitely Victorian and had been very well maintained. You could see it had been painted within the last few years.

"You hoped I'd bring you back here."

"I did," Anthony answered.

"You even expected it."

"Say I hoped."

"No. Be honest. You expected it and would have been disappointed and resentful had I not brought you back here."

"Disappointed, why not? Of course. But resentful?"

"Resentful," Patrick insisted. "It was the way you held on to me, chaining me to you by resentments."

"I didn't," Anthony protested.

"It doesn't matter," Patrick said smiling. He put his arms round him, drew him close, and kissed him. Anthony melted at the shock of the kiss. He had lost the feeling of it even in his dreams. But here it was now. He responded with his entire body.

Patrick drew back. A knife was in his hand. He pressed the point of the knife against the tip of Anthony's nipple. "Do you still get off on fear and pain?"

But there was no need for Anthony to say anything. His body answered. And he said, "I'm afraid I do."

Patrick pricked the nipple with the knife, something he had never done. It felt like when you cut yourself shaving. Anthony gasped more in surprise than in pain. "It's going to be different this time," Patrick said.

"You're not going to hurt me," Anthony said.

"If I am, chained to the four posts of the bed as you will be, you will not be able do anything about it." He spoke and prodded Anthony's nipple with the point of his knife.

"If you want me back, it's a different me you'll be getting. And together we're going to have a different kind of relationship from the one we had."

It did not matter what sort. Anthony knew it: the affinity was there. Nevertheless, "What kind?" he asked. Patrick applied a slight increase in the pressure of the point of his knife to his nipple. "No questions," he said.

Anthony ought not to have stayed in San Francisco. Anthony ought to have returned to Pennsylvania and his comfortable professorship. His book, *Haji Murad, Tolstoy's Brief Epic,* had garnered praise in all the right scholarly publications. It had gotten him a promotion and a raise, and he had already begun to outline the next book, a study of the social implications of Pablo Neruda's love poetry. *Love Inside a Hurricane* he thought he would call it. But he only flew back to Pennsylvania in order to fly out again.

"What are you doing?" Dean Emory said, distraught, as they sat in the faculty lounge instead of Emory's office, pretending something of no great importance was happening.

"I'm quitting," Anthony said with a smile.

"You can't do that," Emory said.

"Yes, I can," Anthony said.

"But it will mean the end of your academic career...for good. Can't you see that? No one will hire you with this kind of thing on your record."

"I'm not worried about that," Anthony responded.

"You're burning your boats. You know that."

"Got a match?"

"I'm frightened for you, Tony, and I have to admit, I'm a bit spooked."

"No need," said Anthony, patting his knee.

"Nevertheless," Emory said.

Anthony was not worried about what he was doing. He was following the instructions Patrick had laid down with a light heart. Within two weeks, the identity it had taken forty-one years to construct had been deconstructed.

Patrick met him at the airport. Anthony had nothing but the few clothes he was wearing. He had no luggage. He gave Patrick his wallet and the few documents he had needed for flying. The proceeds from the sale of his house, furnishings, clothing, books, paintings, CDs, etc. had all been transferred electronically to Patrick's bank account.

A commotion in the mind is not compatible with living successfully and authentically the lives we must from day to day. It is a crippling distraction. What it was in Anthony that made him wish to throw out his entire life and live as the embodiment of another man's will, I do not know. Although I am his biographer, I am not him. I do not understand him. I can guess, though, that there was a commotion in his mind, a commotion of desire, a commotion of dark forces pursuing him from which he was in continuous panic flight. He was a man apparently with perfect balance who was struggling every moment lest he fall.

"I couldn't replace you," Anthony said when Patrick asked him why he had surrendered to him.

"That's too bad," he said, ominously.

"Why?"

"You would have spared yourself what you're in for now."

Anthony thought he did not want Patrick to strike him. Anthony thought he did not want Patrick to humiliate him. Anthony thought he did not want to feel regret at his decision. Anthony thought he did not want to think of it as a sacrifice. Anthony thought he did not want the anger it brought up in him. Anthony thought he did not want to feel anger towards Patrick, that he did not want to hate him. But it was inevitable that he would. It was necessary. Patrick insisted on it by the way he treated him. He had become a skillful master of determining how reality would appear.

He slapped Anthony. Anthony staggered. He punched him in the stomach. Anthony doubled over and held his sides. "I was a fool to come back. I hate you," he said.

"Yes," Patrick laughed. "It will make your obedience that much more valuable. When you obey me it will have nothing to do with whether you want to or not. In fact you probably won't want to." He was laughing as if it were very funny.

It was perverse. The more Anthony did not want to obey him, the more exciting it was to obey him. It showed the force of Patrick's power. It drove Anthony crazy with excitement to submit to him. Anthony thought he wanted to resist him, to vanquish him with the strength of his resistance. But he was mistaken. His resistance was the essential prelude to his defeat.

Of course, resistance was the necessary condition for submission. Patrick knew how to do with Anthony what he liked. Moreover, it seemed he really did not have to do anything. His predominance was part of the nature of things. Anthony could do nothing but obey him. Patrick's power overwhelmed him. Anthony was the slave of unshakably intense desire.

First his mind went blank. Then it began to re-form. He was not aware when it happened, but he realized it had happened when his mind became still, quiet, and constant, hovering endlessly over him like a cloudless blue sky on a comfortable summer day. His mind was no longer his root. Patrick was his root. Patrick was the soil he grew in. Without Patrick he would be a plucked grass blade or some-such.

Without understanding the strange affinity between them, without sensing the intangible that united them, it will be impossible to understand how their diurnal interactions had the force and significance they did, for they were after all, the same routine things that make up the mass of lives, the daily chores, routines, habits, and obligations that most of us share, despite what else separates us.

It was through his mind that Patrick entered Anthony. Once that entrance had been accomplished, however, Anthony's mind was of no more use. But it was that act of possession that Patrick re-created, when it was translated to the corporeal realm, every time he hovered bodily above Anthony, piercing his eyes, penetrating him, stretching above him and inside him rigidly, suspended over him, inside him like iron, undulating fiercely or locked in stillness, until orgasms tore at them like vicious dogs and they clawed at each other with teeth and fingers and nails.

THE END

WANT FREE COPIES OF MY BOOKS?
Just visit my blog and download free copies of my books:
http://gideon-elliot.awesomeauthors.org/gideon-elliot/

Here is a sample from another story you may enjoy:

6-BOOK BOX SET
My Fair
MASTER
Gay Erotic Romance
GIDEON ELLIOT

In Antibes, just outside the walls of the old city, on the rue de Recherche, where boys lean against the wall wearing hardly more than their dark summer tans and wait for free-spending tourists to notice them, there's an absinthe bar in the basement of a shop that sells gourmet olive oil, scented vinegar, hand-crafted kitchen implements, mixed herbs, exotic pastas, and fancy soap during the day mostly to Americans and Germans who have a particular fondness for their kitchens and their bathrooms and the money to indulge it.

Looking like a van Gogh in yellow, blue, olive, and red, the assomoir is open after the shop upstairs has long been shut. Patrons come and leave through an ill-lit side entrance negotiating a flight of steep and twisting wooden steps. The pale and dirty stucco walls are coated with a red stain cast by the bare exit bulb stuck in the ceiling.

It is a quiet place with marble table tops and amber light bulbs. Water carafes with little spigots stand on chrome feet at the center of the tables. Sometimes some of the boys from outside lean against the bar nursing a drink and look blank, waiting for something to happen. I had taken to hanging out there nearly every night, either passing through just for one drink at the bar, or sometimes settling at one of the round tables to write or to sketch. Every now and then I'd gaze at the boys, admiring their youth, but since I never would consent to be a paying customer, none of them had eyes for me. And all I was left with was to wonder at their unreflecting inwardness.

As I was about to leave one evening in early August, hoping to take a walk along the ramparts overlooking the blue Mediterranean before complete nightfall, a young American, a good looking sunned and tousle-haired boy of around nineteen with sparkling, questing, needy eyes asked if he could sit down at my table.

"Sure," I said.

"I've seen you several times before this," he said, fastening his gaze upon me and catching mine in his.

I looked him over to see if I could recognize him, but had no recollection of having seen him before and was quite certain, given his good looks and lean but well-wrought frame apparent under his loose-hanging striped boatman shirt and faded jeans, that I would have if I had.

He smiled showing perfect teeth.

"You're not one of them," I said.

"What?"

"You're not one of the beach boys that hang around the street at night."

"No," he said. "I'm not."

"I can tell," I said.

"How?" he asked smiling. "By my eyes?"

"No," I said. "By the loose hang of your clothes."

He blushed.

"Who are you?" I said.

He told me his name.

"I've never seen you here before," I said. But I recognized his name. "Your father," I began, but he interrupted me.

"Yes," he said, and I knew all I needed to know and from politeness moved quickly away from the subject.

"Have we met?" I asked.

"I don't expect you'd have noticed me," he said modestly. "The last time I saw you, it was at the Picasso museum and you were totally absorbed by the de Stael exhibition. A few days before that, I saw you with a German boy having coffee in a café above the beach."

I winced. I remembered him.

He blushed when he added, "the only thing I think you could see was his eyes. You both were gazing into each other's eyes to the exclusion of everything else."

"It happens," I said, "when I get lucky," I added, not without irony as we continued to mirror each other's gaze.

He registered the ambiguity but proceeded without letting it sabotage him.

"I want it to happen to me," he said, and blushed again, nevertheless
looking straight at me.

"You do?" I said.

"With you," he said.

"With me," I said, quizzically.

"Yes," he said, determined not to be put off.

"Have you ever had absinthe?"

"I've only read about it," he said, shaking his head.

"Laurent," I said to the barman, signaling for a glass of La Muse Verte for the boy and a refill for me.

He brought them and I added water to each.

"You can put sugar in if you like," I said, "but I don't."

"Then I won't either," he said." I want to do things the way you do."

I looked at him.

"I have a sixth sense," he said, as we tilted our glasses towards each other, and our eyes began their slow embrace.

"I want you to make me your boy," he said. "I want to belong to you."

"Do you know what that means?" I said.

"I think I do," he said, "and I want to know how it feels." His voice was deep and sweet and slow.

I couldn't tell who was taking control of whom as we gazed into each other's eyes.

"Have you ever made love to a man?" I asked.

"No," he answered.

"Do you want to?"

"If the man is you," he said.

If you enjoyed this sample then look for **My Fair Master**.

Also by this Author

From the Author

WANT FREE COPIES OF MY BOOKS?
Just visit my blog and download free copies of my books:

http://gideon-elliot.awesomeauthors.org/gideon-elliot/

Check my page on Amazon and my blog for Updates and interesting info.

Author Central - http://www.amazon.com/Gideon-Elliot/e/B00DUYBEQC

If you enjoyed any of my books then please share the love and click like on my books in Amazon.

If you write me a review and send me an email I will send you a free book, or many.
(Just know that these emails are filtered by my publisher.)

Good news is always welcome.

One Last Thing, For Kindle Readers...

When you turn the page, Kindle will give you the opportunity to rate this book and share your thoughts on Facebook and Twitter. If you enjoyed my writings, would you please take a few seconds to let your friends know about it? Because... when they enjoy they will be grateful to you and so will I.

Thank You!

Gideon Elliot
gideon_elliot@awesomeauthors.org

About the Author

Gideon Elliot was born in 1981 in Wichita, Kansas.

He grew up in San Francisco and spends the greater part of the year, now, on one of the Cyclades Islands in Greece where he runs a jazz café, paints, writes poetry, and swims.

He has a small apartment in Greenwich Village, where he stays from the middle of November to the end of April and, during those months, manages an erotic men's clothing shop. He began writing erotic fiction at the age of fifteen.

You may also like the books by these authors:

A GAY ROMANCE STORY

Snowbird Romance

DICK PARKER

I think I may have the best job in the entire world. I go camping for a living. Yes, I get paid to go camping and write about it.

I have a degree in marketing and creative writing. When I graduated with my BA degree I had no idea what I wanted to do so I went back to school and got my Masters. I put off becoming a big person for another couple of years.

During my college years I was pretty average. I drank my share of beer and smoked a little grass and I dated a few girls. When I went back to work on my Masters I met a woman in the same program and soon we were living together. She was a beautiful young woman and had a killer body, but our sex life was not real great. She was hot and horny all the time but it took a lot to get me in the mood. I always thought it was stress from school or something like that but I think deep down I knew I just wasn't into her.

We struggled through nearly two years of a relationship and she finally threw me out. Actually it came as a relief.

I finished school and got hired as a feature writer for a national magazine called Camping Association of America. It was a magazine for and about camping. I worked for about a year and then one day I pitched an idea to the boss.

"What we need is a camping critic," I said. "We send someone out to check a place out and then write it up in the magazine. Of course the marketing department will let the place know what's coming and sell them advertising."

The boss liked the idea and six months later I was the new roving camper. They bought me a nice motor home and turned me loose. I'd set out and pick a campground and stay for a few days. Then I'd write a piece, email it in and the sales department would take over. The plan worked like a charm.

Our advertising revenues soared and the sales of the magazine doubled. People liked to read about the places they were considering going to.

And I became a professional camper. And I got paid a shit-load of money for it. I had the perfect job.

The nice part of my job was that in the summer I'd stay in the northern part of the country. I camped from coast to coast in states like

Oregon, North Dakota, Montana, Minnesota and Wisconsin. Then when the snow came, I became a snowbird and headed south. I camped all across the bottom half of the country until winter was over.

I was in a campground near Galveston, Texas enjoying a beautiful day when the weather started turning ugly. I listened to the radio and a bad storm was approaching that would bring rain and wind. They warned of near hurricane conditions, so I cleared up my outdoor furniture and battened down the hatches.

The storm hit late in the afternoon. My campsite was just about a hundred yards off Galveston Bay. The bay turned to an angry sea and waves crashed up on the seawall. I was glad I had a nice big safe motor home to keep me warm and dry.

I was working on a piece for the magazine about the last place I'd camped when I happened to glance out the window. I couldn't believe my eyes.

There was a kid on a bicycle straining against the wind trying to get to a campsite a little way from me. The rain was coming down in sheets and the wind was whipping him around so he nearly flew off his bike.

"He's nuts," I said to myself.

I watched as he got off the bike. He was wearing a backpack and had another strapped to the old bike. He opened the other pack and pulled a nylon pup tent out of it.

I looked at him and he looked like he must be homeless. His hair was long and needed a barber very badly. He had a scraggly beard and was wearing some old stained shorts, a tee shirt and plastic flip-flops that he probably got from a Dollar Store for a buck.

He tried to get the tent spread out and just when he'd get it the wind would whip it up and he'd have to start over. It wasn't going to happen.

If you enjoyed this sample then look for <u>Snowbird Romance</u>.

DEXTER CHASE

FULL

Gay Disclosure

NAUGHTY COLLEGE MEN

The dean walked into the staff common room looking very smug, accompanied by what all the staff members guessed to be a new staff member. They checked him out; he was an even, six footer, built like an American Football player, impressive. The staff realized straight away that something momentous was going to be announced. For a long time, the dean had walked around with a beaten look. Not surprising really, school discipline had gone to the dogs and it had overflowed onto the college campus. Successive governments made it impossible to punish students resulting to anarchy in the lecture rooms. Lecturers had virtually ceased to try teaching and usually sat reading or processing further qualifications while the students did whatever they wanted. They came to college mainly because that was a good place to meet all their friends and it was warm and dry, and most importantly kept them out of the workplace. Tom Howard spent more time interviewing new staff and appointing new dorm supervisors than he did in improving the education department's directives.

"Ladies and gentlemen, good morning."

They all chorused the reply and Tom, grinning like an idiot continued, "I would like to introduce to you the new CDO and that stands for *College Disciplinary Officer*. Jarek Howard is my younger brother so this appointment gives me double pleasure. The government has at last acted on the discipline problem and they have chosen us to try the new program. All and I mean all restrictions on punishment are lifted. Jarek will be able to do anything he likes to students sent to him for punishment. If a student refuses to accept the punishment, Jarek will refer him to me and the student will be sent down and incarcerated in the first of the junior prisons. It is where discipline will be enforced by men whom we have called *goons* in a previous regime. A female CDO is currently in training and shall be with us within the next month."

Tom went on describing how the system would work in practice.

"I am appointing a new batch of dorm supervisors from the two senior years and Jarek will always have two with him to witness punishment and if he wishes they can take part. Most punishment will take place in the CDO's room but if he considers it beneficial, he may interrupt a lecture and conduct the punishment in the lecture room of the student concerned. I will be making announcements during the assembly tomorrow morning. I'll be posting notices on all college boards. I am also going to introduce a uniform code which again will be strictly enforced."

There were gasps at that since no one had ever tried to put college students in uniform.

"Please, try not to send him too many students at once, just the worst cases. I'm sure that the numbers will very quickly drop to near zero because Jarek has told me what he intends to do. No student, however bold, will want to see him twice and I understand the female CDO will be equally as awful. I will leave Jarek with you for an hour and then he will spend the remainder of today briefing our new supervisors."

The staff bombarded Jarek with questions and at the end of the hour could hardly wait to get to their classrooms for the last day of anarchy. Jarek took over the double room allocated to him and was soon sitting with twelve boys who were the dean's original appointees but who had resigned because they considered it impossible to do their job.

"I am going to make this easy for you. I know you are all serious students who excel in sports and academics, so asking you to witness some of the actions I am going to take may not appeal to you. I am going to tell you now and it is no shame if you want to leave. I am allowed to cane bad boys, but I am going to make most of my punishments embarrassing and humiliating. That means the student will be made to strip and depending on his attitude and crime, will be made to carry out degrading sexual acts. Nothing is forbidden so I can go to being the complete hog and even use anal intercourse as a punishment. I will, on convenient occasions, use you boys to render the punishment. Of course, you will only be delivering it not receiving it. Now, if any of you thinks you can't handle that may leave."

No one moved.

"Good. Now first thing's first, from now on nothing you see or hear concerning my job is ever discussed with other people. If you betray that trust you will receive my worst punishment."

Still, no one moved.

"Alright, I want you all to strip naked and then get an erection."

If you enjoyed this sample then look for **Full Gay Disclosure**.

Wrong Place. Wrong Time

Caged Sanctuary

Chris Johns' Gay Compilation, Vol. 5

People can change in a matter of seconds, forbidden desires you never knew were inside can erupt when you give in to the hunger and leave inhibitions behind. What starts as lust can turn you into something else. Better or worse…

Freedom is taken away by lies, and love and innocence is lost or willingly given. Cages become a sanctuary or a nightmare. Deals are struck but ulterior motives arise. Choices are made but consequences prove more than what the body can take and weaknesses are taken advantage of. These are the stories of the men that are faced with intimate experiences that can break a man but choose to go on and push themselves to their limits and submit to the heights of pleasure. Their hearts are sad but their body enjoys every minute of it and craves for more.

Things never felt so good to be at the **wrong place at the wrong time**.

This collection of stories includes:

Tremors In The Interrogation Room
Prisoner Of His Heart
A Trade For A Trade
Payback Scandal
Erotic Expense

If you enjoyed this sample then look for <u>Wrong Place.</u> <u>Wrong Time</u>.

Son Swap

ANGUS MACGREGOR

HOT GAY EROTICA

Walking over the top of the ridge, Paul Gibson smiled as the blue vista of the Pacific Ocean greeted his eyes. Sam came up behind him and laid a heavy hand on his shoulder. Both men were panting. The last hundred yards of the hiking trail had been practically vertical, but it paid off in a spectacular fashion. The view stretched from Seaside all the way south to Tillamook. The canopy of Douglas fir and Sitka spruce had opened up to reveal a turquoise sky that blended in with the vast azure of the ocean far below.

"Okay," Sam panted. "You were right, buddy. This was definitely worth the five miles. Holy shit! It's so beautiful."

"I know. When Cole and I came up here last spring, I was pretty blown away so I definitely wanted you to see it."

The men stood on the edge of the cliff. The wind blew their hair and thin hiking shorts around like sails. The air was cool to their sweaty chests, bare and beaded with sweat. It was a hot day for the north Oregon coast. They had passed only one other hiker on the trail and he was headed back down to the trail head. Paul took a long drink of water and passed the bottle to Sam who finished it. Paul took another step closer to the edge of the cliff and pulled out his dick and sent a long golden stream over the rim toward the crashing surf far surging beneath.

"Look out below," he bellowed laughing. Sam pulled out his dick and joined the party, two yellow arcs glistening in the sunlight.

"This is one of those moments when I just couldn't imagine being a woman. I love pissing outside so easy like this."

"I'm with you, buddy. Add that to my list of gratitude for being a dude. I'm sure there's plenty of wonderful things about being a girl, but since I really don't get it, I'm happy to be pissing into the wind with you right now," Sam said with a chuckle. "Damn, this cool breeze is giving me a chub."

"You always have a chub, buddy," Paul said, shaking his penis but leaving it hanging out of his shorts. "Maybe we should do the hike back naked? You brave enough?"

"Sure. We've ran into naked hikers before. No one ever says anything. It's Oregon for God's sake."

"So true."

"We should bring our boys up here and see if they would go for a naked hike. Would be fun to see them out here like that. You want some jerky?" Paul dug a baggie full of beef jerky from his backpack and passed some to Sam. It was sweet and spicy. The men chewed the beef and continued to point to landmarks and enjoy the brilliance of the perfect afternoon.

"So often when you get out here, it fogs up and you can hardly see anything. This day is amazing," Sam said with a mouth full of jerky. "You gonna stand there all day with your dick hanging out?"

"Yeah, I might. You sure seem to like staring at my Johnson."

Sam laughed. "You and I have been staring at one another for quite a while now. You'd think we'd be used to it. But I still enjoy the view whenever I get a chance."

Paul pulled the man toward him in a close embrace. Sam's skin felt warm and soft against his own. Sam's dark furry belly pressed close against his smooth one. Their faces were close, lips and noses only separated by a tiny space. Paul reached up and touched Sam's jaw. The dark stubble was prickly to his fingers but for some reason, this made his penis swell. Sam's rough hand gripped his shaft and ran his thumb across the piss slit, now slick with precum. Paul's hand slid inside Sam's shorts and gripped the man's thick, solid cock. The full bush felt soft and ticklish to his hand. He slid his hand around the man's sack and let the plum sized testicles roll in his palm. His breath increased and he closed his eyes as Sam's soft, thick lips brushed against his.

"Man, this never gets old, my friend," Sam whispered against his lips.

"I know, bro. It just keeps getting better…"

If you enjoyed this sample then look for Son Swap.

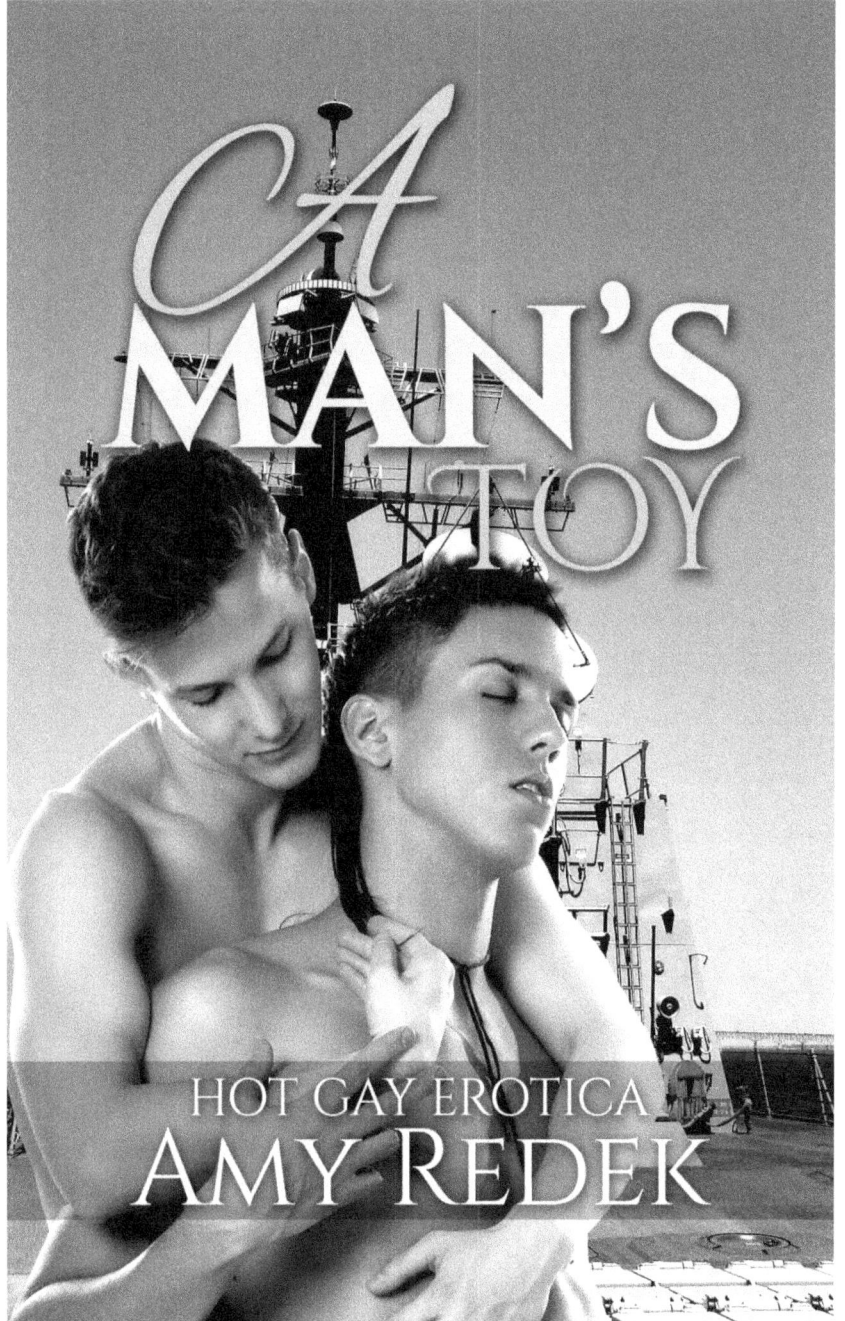

A MAN'S TOY

HOT GAY EROTICA
AMY REDEK

I've still got the toy I was given when I was born and in growing up found that other boys had the same toy that I had, and in the process of getting older, still played with our toys.

I never knew my father because he was in the army and was killed somewhere in Northern India while serving his country. I was born a month after he had left and so it was only my mother that looked after me until I was able to look after myself. Which was quite early considering that mom, when I was old enough, around four years old, was to be looked after in a small crèche while she went to work in a munitions factory at the outbreak of what was known as "The Second World War".

I was taken there in the morning before she went to work and collected me in the early evening to take me home to feed, bathe and put me to bed, only having a Sunday to spend the whole day with me. I cannot say that I remember much of this, only one thing stands out clear was having to spend one night in a bomb shelter and was told later that I had cried so much that we never went into one again. We were lucky to be on the outskirt of London and so didn't have to suffer the bombing that the capital suffered.

It was a good thing that when I was five, I only had to be taken to school on that first day and from there on, went on my own and returned home well before mom came in from work.

As I grew older, I began to learn how to cook a meal so that she didn't have to worry about me being home alone and I think she appreciated having her dinner cooked for her. She had been heartbroken when she was informed that her husband had died in battle but still had me to remember him by and didn't marry again until I was sixteen.

I didn't like her choice and so stayed out of the house as much as possible, for I could never call him dad or father. I had left school at fifteen and found work as an errand boy and with this arrival of another man in the house, found a job for the evenings. This was in a hotel in the city and would start at mid-day until eight in the evening, travelling backwards and forwards by the underground train. I liked Saturdays, for they usually had functions there and so would do the extra hours until it finished and would then sleep in the cloakroom and work the Sunday morning until the afternoon, where I would then go to a cinema to watch whatever film was being shown before going home.

It was during this time that I learned that even though the country would be stopping conscription into the army sometime in the future, I would still be liable to being called up when I was eighteen. Now I could volunteer to join either the army or navy before the time arrived of my eighteenth birthday or enter the Merchant Navy, though that would mean being in there for seven years as opposed to only two in the army. The Royal Navy was seven years too, but more restrictive than the Merchant Navy, so that was what I planned to join.

I got the necessary papers finally and it took some time to get my mom to sign them, even though she knew that by me going to sea I would soon be leaving home, but also didn't want me to join the army and maybe having to go out and fight like my father had, so she signed them.

Now with the man she had married and herself, she always left home around seven thirty in the morning while I stayed in bed until they had gone before getting up. Seeing to my own breakfast, as not having to be at the hotel until mid-day, I would always see what the postman dropped through our letterbox. The day finally came when there was one brown envelope from the government that I knew would contain the order for me to do my National Service. This was three months before I would be eighteen, and so I wrote on the envelope that the person this letter was for, no longer lived at this address and posted it back on my way to take the signed paperwork to the office where they would see me to joining the Merchant Navy.

As I was still only seventeen, I would have to attend a navy school, which was at Gravesend, and they would let me know by letter the date to attend there. It was to take a course of six weeks and on passing, would be allocated to a ship. It was a month before this letter arrived giving me the date to attend this school, which was another four weeks later. This meant that I would then be eighteen by the time I finished at the school and would therefore not be classed as a boy rating. Oh, it was the catering department that I had applied for as opposed to being a deck hand for if I would be at sea in a winter time, it would be warmer being on the inside of the ship than out on deck.

In the meantime, another letter had come from the government asking mom where I might be contacted for my joining the army. She showed me this and didn't quite know what to say in reply. I told her to just say that I had since joined the Merchant Navy. So that cleared that problem.

I'd already given in my notice to the hotel that I would soon be leaving to join the navy and had a little party given me on my last day working there as I would on the following Monday have to report to the Gravesend school. Mom was in tears on that day when I left at six a.m., consoling her by saying that I would be back in six weeks time before having to finally go to sea.

I duly turned up at the school on time, following others with their suitcases and saw that it looked like a prison that we would be spending the next six weeks in. In fact, it had once been a prison. One for women. There were twenty of us that lined up once we were inside and with me being at least a foot taller than the others, was made the senior of half of the group with another tall boy being the senior of the other half. We were to keep control of the others during our stay there. What a dump. Ten of us in a small dismal, filthy room that had five double bunks for us to sleep in. It only had one window that was filthy so the light had to be on even when it was daylight outside.

It definitely seemed like a prison, being woken up in the morning by the officer in charge of us, making a racket in the room and shouting out, "Hands off cocks and hands on socks" every morning at five thirty. This would give us thirty minutes to fight at the washbasins, three of them, to wash and clean our teeth before breakfast at six. Seven o'clock we would be in a class to then be shown what was expected of us.

How to make a bed navy fashion, which wasn't far off how I had been making mine for quite a few years. How to lay a table for meals, the same here too and so on. The names of a ship's interior: the floor being the deck, the ceiling a deckhead, the walls being bulkheads and many other names used aboard. The pecking order of the officers and of the stripes on their shoulders and what we had to wear when doing a daily chore and the change when we were seeing to passengers.

It was bad at first but we all got used to it and we all did well with our final tests at what we had been taught, and I got a good report from the officer that had been teaching us, rating me as excellent and top of our class. On our last day at the school, I was told that because I would then be eighteen by the time it came for me to report to a ship, I would be rated as being a steward, and would inside a week or too, know what ship I was to join and where.

I think we were all relieved to be leaving this prison to return to our homes to await our letters. Mom was pleased to see me though I wasn't sure about the man who had married her. I think he was glad that I would soon be leaving for good, little did he know that there would be times when I had ship's leave to spend there.

Though he did give me a present on my birthday, me thinking at first that he was taking the piss when I saw that it was a bible. But then he showed me how to open the inside cover that would be the ideal place to keep any money I had for if things were to be stolen on board ship, a bible would be the last thing that would be taken, and he was right. For things did tend to suddenly disappear from our cabins when in port and yet my bible was left alone. So overall, it wasn't a bad little party we had to celebrate me now being regarded as a man.

It wouldn't be long before I would learn how other men who not only played with their toys, but also what they did with them.

If you enjoyed this sample then look for **A Man's Toy.**

WANT FREE COPIES OF MY BOOKS?

Just visit my blog and download free copies of my books:

http://gideon-elliot.awesomeauthors.org/gideon-elliot/

www.ingramcontent.com/pod-product-compliance
Lightning Source LLC
Chambersburg PA
CBHW071328130626
46556CB00004B/1804